My Little Pony
Holiday Talent Show

by Claire Kinkaid
illustrated by Carlo LoRaso

HARPER FESTIVAL
An Imprint of HarperCollinsPublishers

It was holiday time in Ponyville.
Snow dotted the streets outside the ponies' houses.
The sun shone brightly.

Pinkie Pie wanted to do something extra-special
to celebrate the holidays. But what?
Maybe Sweetie Belle could help her think of something.

"Can you think of an extra-special way for all of us to celebrate the holidays this year?" Pinkie Pie asked her friend.
"How about a holiday bake-off?" suggested Sweetie Belle.
"That would be yummy!"

Pinkie Pie thought a bake-off could be fun.
But she wasn't very good at baking.
"I don't know," she said as she left. "I'll think about it. Thank you
for the delicious cupcake! You are such a good baker."

At Fancy Fashions Boutique, Rainbow Dash was putting up her winter window display. Pinkie Pie stopped to admire a beautiful red-and-white-striped scarf with sparkles.

"Hello, Pinkie Pie," said Rainbow Dash.
"Are you looking for a special present? Come inside!"

"I'm trying to think of an extra-special way
for all of us to celebrate the holidays this year," said Pinkie Pie.
"Do you have any ideas, Rainbow Dash?"

Rainbow Dash wrapped the striped scarf around Pinkie Pie
and put a sparkly hat on her head. "There's your answer,"
she said proudly. "A holiday fashion parade!"

Pinkie Pie laughed when she saw herself in the mirror.
A fashion show would be lots of fun. But what if she tripped
on stage? She wasn't a talented fashion model.

"Maybe," said Pinkie Pie as she left the shop. "I'll think about it.
Thanks for the scarf and hat! You are a great fashion designer!"

Pinkie Pie walked along the main street past the
La-Ti-Da Hair and Spa. When she reached Toola-Roola's art studio,
she stopped and stared at a beautiful painting in the window.
"Wow!" exclaimed Pinkie Pie.

Toola-Roola appeared from around the corner. "Happy holidays,
Pinkie Pie," said Toola-Roola. "The painting is for you!"
Pinkie Pie smiled and hugged her friend. "Thank you, Toola-Roola!
You are such a wonderful artist!"

Suddenly, Pinkie Pie had an idea. "I've got it!" shouted Pinkie Pie.
"See you later! I have to go!"

"Wait!" cried Toola-Roola.
"Got what? Where are you going?"

Pinkie Pie spent the rest of the day planning.

Then she gathered all of her friends at the wishing well to tell them her great idea. "Let's have a holiday talent show!" she said. All the ponies cheered.

Ponyville buzzed with excitement for weeks.
Finally the night of the talent show arrived.
Backstage, Sweetie Belle decorated the refreshments.
Scootaloo practiced her famous triple-whirl trick on her scooter.

Rainbow Dash put the last touches on all the costumes.
There were sparkly hats for everyone!
Cheerilee handed out the fliers she had made.
Toola-Roola finished painting a big mural on the stage.

Starsong opened the show with a holiday song.

All the ponies joined in on the chorus!

When the talent show was over, Starsong made a special announcement. "We'd like to thank one special pony for showing her talent tonight, too."

Pinkie Pie looked around. She hadn't planned for this.

"Thank you, Pinkie Pie, for having the talent
to recognize the special talents in each of us.
And for making this the best holiday celebration ever!"
Pinkie Pie blushed and took a bow with all of her friends.